For Mom

Published in 2004 by Simply Read Books Inc. www.simplyreadbooks.com

CATALOGUING IN PUBLICATION DATA

. . . .

WELLER, DUNCAN, 1965-
    SPACESNAKE/ DUNCAN WELLER, AUTHOR AND ILLUSTRATOR

ISBN 1-894965-09-4

    I. TITLE.

PS8645.E45S65 2004   jC813'.6   C2004-900031-4

. . . .

Copyright © 2004 by Duncan Weller www.duncanweller.com

Printed in the USA

10 9 8 7 6 5 4 3 2 1

Book Design by Elisa Gutiérrez

Black and white scans by ScanLab

Duncan Weller

Spacesnake

Always love people and use things,
Never use people and love things.

TURN THE PAGE!

SIMPLY READ BOOKS

From the depths of deepest space,

from the vast reaches of the most lonely emptiness came something dark and terrible.

The thing was a silent monster with quick-firing rockets and a nasty nuclear power drive hidden in its belly.

It swirled its metal body at gas-splintering speeds, had inter-twirling fibre wires for menacing muscle and a coal-fired furnace for heat.

With heavy-duty battery boxes it could snap-change its direction like a whip, without warning.

It was a mechanical monstrosity, a sinister string of metal tubes and riveted plates.

Its flight was aimless, its purpose no good, and the only results of its despicable deeds were destructive.

It was a *Spacesnake*!

Many double moons ago, the Spacesnake headed toward an asteroid ring. The Asterians who lived there were unaware of its stealthy approach.

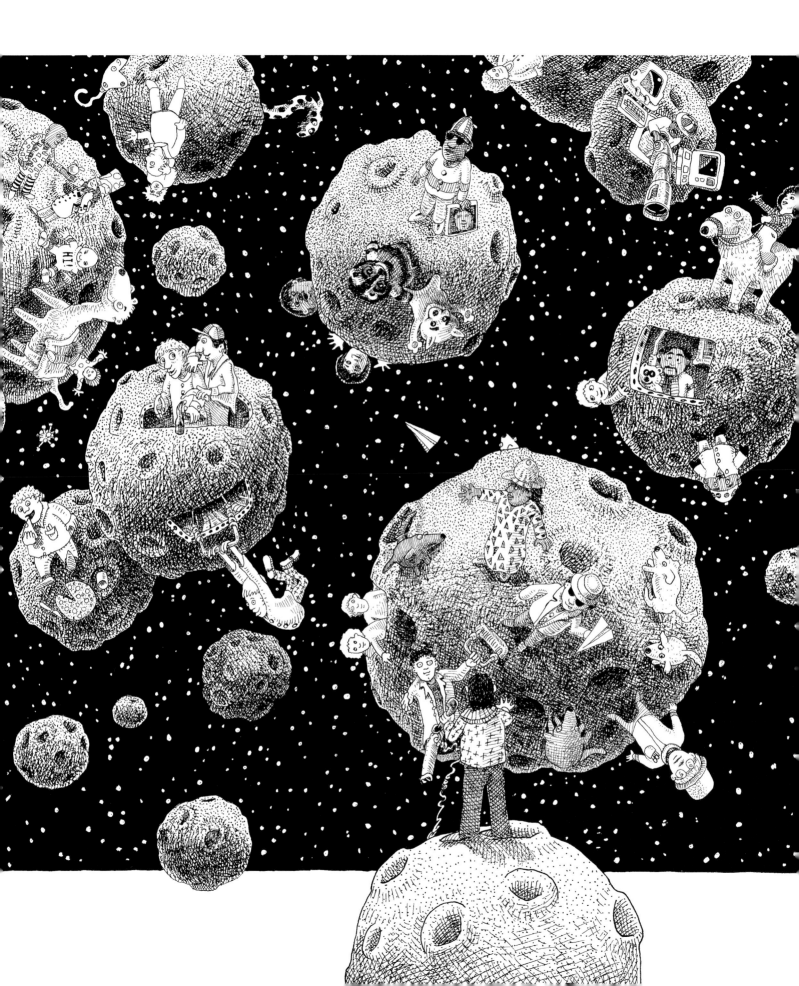

The Spacesnake powered down from a loud rumble to a hum, from a hum to a whisper, and from a whisper to no sound at all. It curled itself up behind two small asteroids, then stretched its head forward and had a good look around.

The Spacesnake waited at a distance and watched the Asterians having fun on their small worlds of low gravity. But most Asterians were hidden from the Spacesnake, because they never roamed outside their asteroids. Instead, they spent all their time with their Interpets.

The Interpet was a special machine each Asterian had in their asteroid. The Interpet was a television, telephone, computer, video eye, DVD player, HDCD crossover, a 9-wing game blaster, and QLP-3D-ZXer Vision 5, with roll-around plasma infiltrators and quadraphonic sound. It was inter-everything. For many Asterians the Interpet was their universe.

Some were happier with their Interpet because they were too shy to meet other people and too afraid of what might appear from the great depths of space. Every once in a while some strange object or phenomenon would fly by and scare everyone. As one Asterian had said, "You just don't know what's out there."

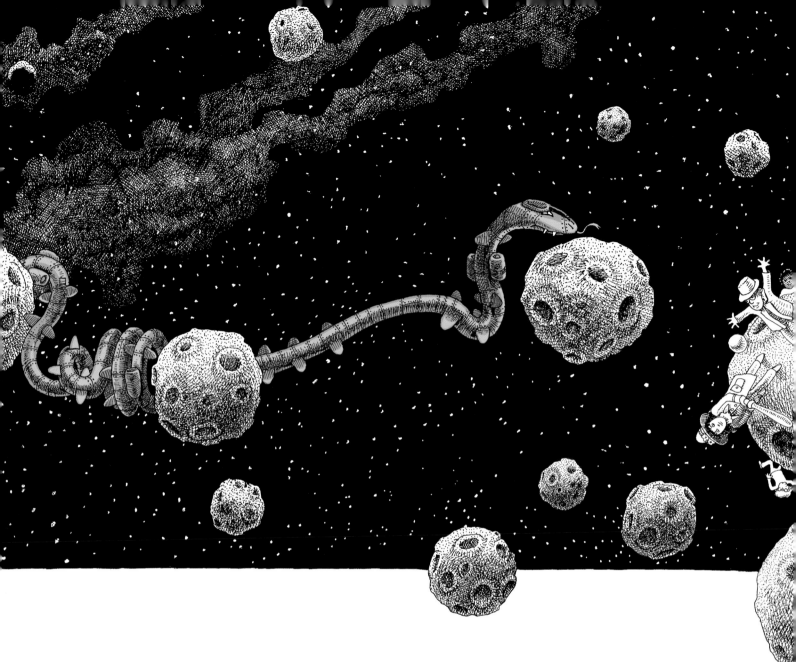

Out there, watching the Asterians intently, was a giant
mechanical monster — the Spacesnake.

The Spacesnake swooped and swiveled around the asteroids with just the right twist and speed so as not to be seen. It swiffed under one asteroid, swung past another, coiled up behind one more and snuck up behind the last.

Then the Spacesnake did the terrible things it had come to do.

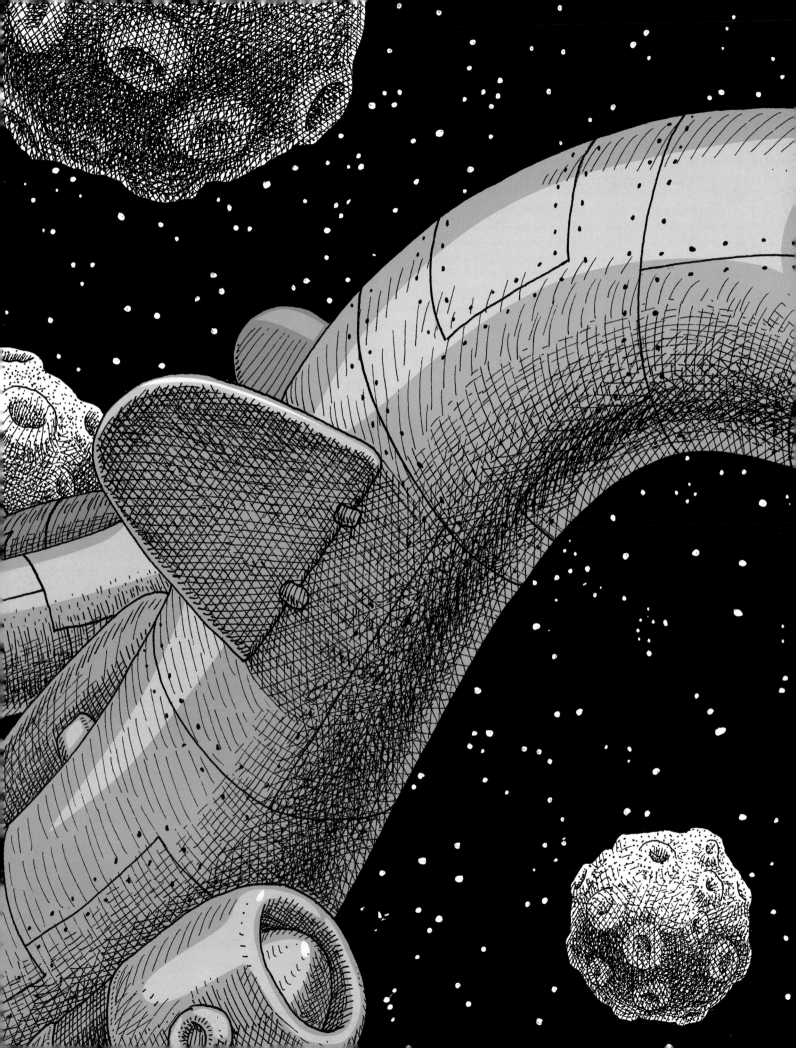

A frightening metal-scraping hiss-shaking roar from the echoing depths of the snake's burning throat blasted out across the Asterians' homes.

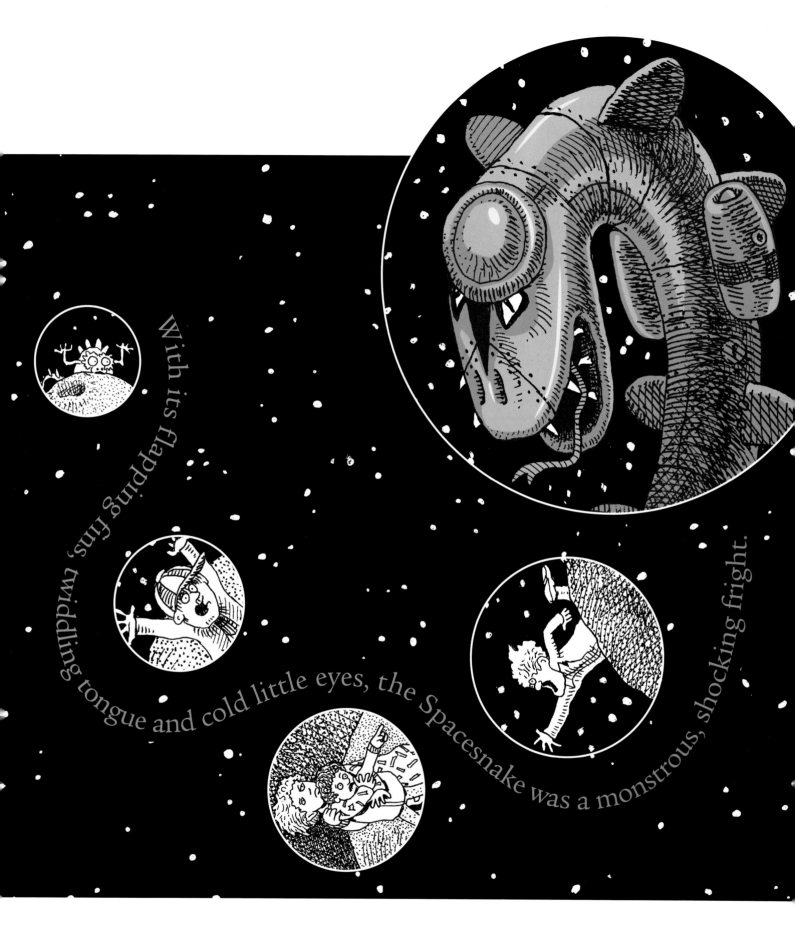

With its flapping fins, twiddling tongue and cold little eyes, the Spacesnake was a monstrous, shocking fright.

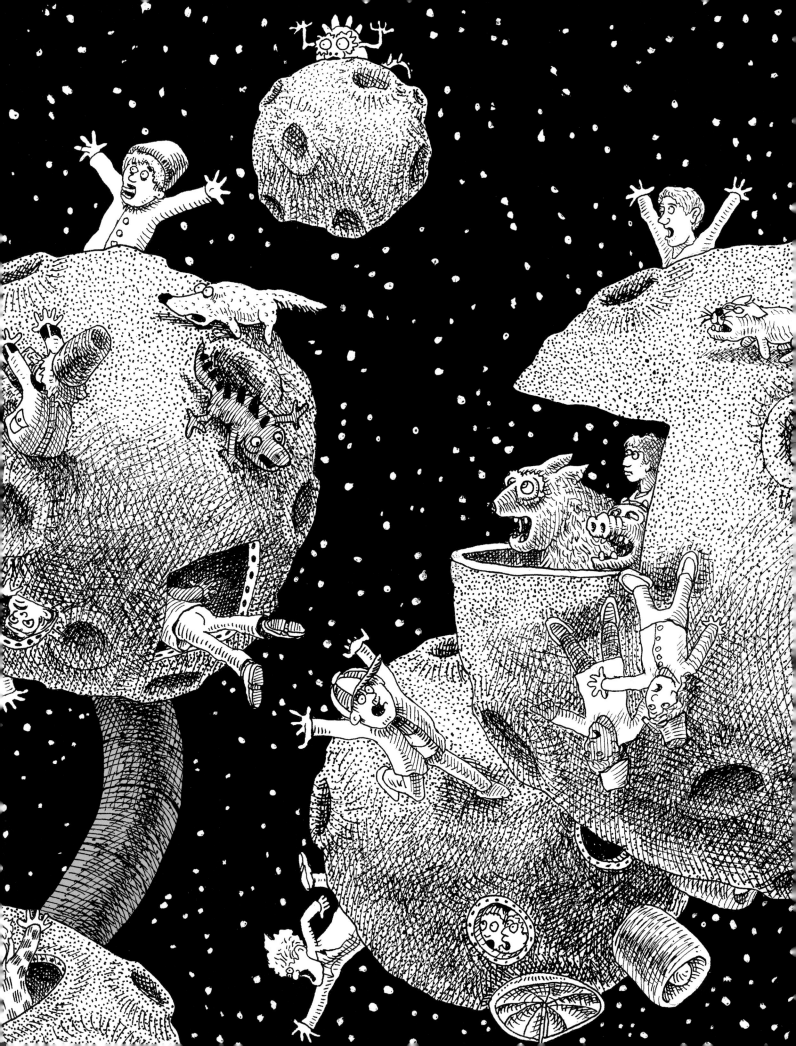

The Spacesnake
made some
Asterians run,
some scream,
some wish they
had never been
born, and…

… it made some cry.

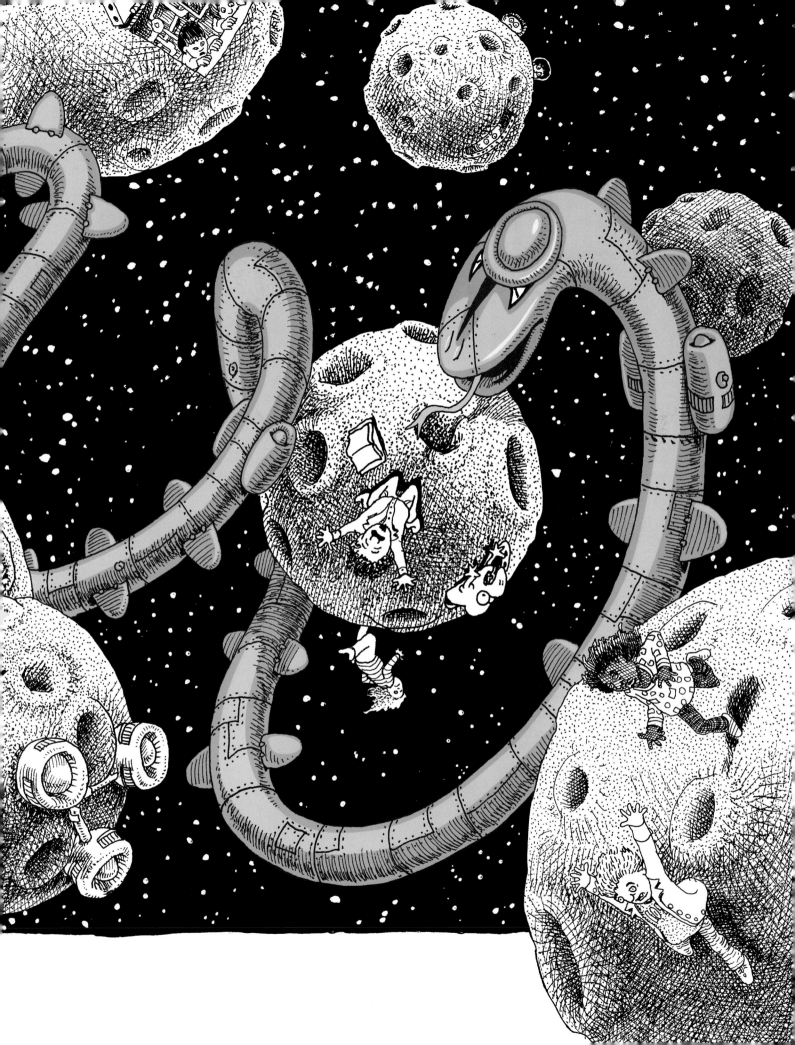

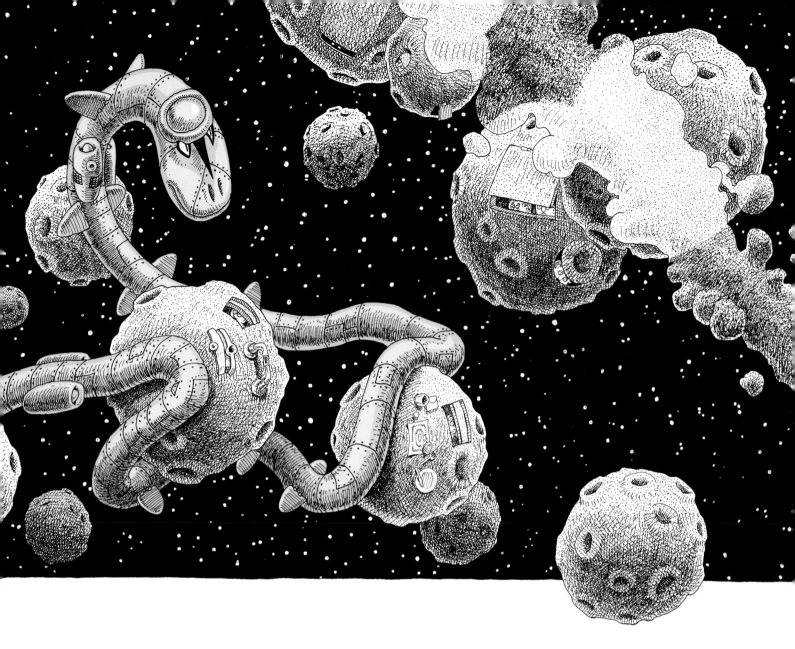

When everyone had fled and
hid themselves inside, the
Spacesnake stopped its
awful hissing and shaking.

The Spacesnake hovered
over the asteroids, looking
fierce and proud. It waited
for anyone brave enough
to peek their heads out.

While the Spacesnake waited,
a strange cloud floated by.
The cloud was filled with the
mouth-watering smells of
goodies freshly baked.

So the Spacesnake slithered
away to follow the cloud until
he found the goodies. Cookies,
bread, and muffins!

From the cookie asterbake.

While terror raged amongst the asteroids, there lay a sleepy boy who thought it was a double moon day like any other double moon day. When he woke up, he was completley unaware that everyone was hiding in fear.

The boy climbed slowly and sleepily down the ladder to his lower room feeling less inclined to play with his Interpet than usual. Ordinarily, every double moon day he would look out his window to see if the world outside might be more interesting compared to the world inside his Interpet.

On this double moon day, to his great surprise, it was!

He saw something so unusual that he had to show it to everyone.

So the boy turned on his Interpet and aimed the video lens outside his window. Then he used the auto connect to transmit the view from his window to all the Asterians.

The boy turned on the lights to shine a powerful beam onto the scene of a crime in action on the Asterbake. The hatch on top of the mechanical Spacesnake's head was open. Nearby sat a startled thief, munching on a cookie.

Everyone hiding in their asteroids could now see that they had been terrified by a nun more liken to a worm than a snake.

It was so unlike a snake, it was hard to believe it could be. But it was not a monster after all

With jeering and jibes, with laughter and roars, the Asterians burst open their doors, threw open their windows, and clambered away in one big, howling, noisy fuss. They hissed with anger, smiled with relief, stuck out their tongues in mockery, booed, pointed, jockled, and danced jigs.

They were so relieved that the big mechanical monster was just a runt.

They were angry because they had been tricked and falsely frightened.

They were ashamed that they had run away so quickly.

They told each other that the next time a monster came, they would all be braver.

So the Asterians cast out the little runt into empty space.

The little snake took the controls inside the Spacesnake shell and fled into deep space. The little snake ran its nuclear powered electric furnace fired rockets across the galaxy. Eventually, it soaked up its uranium, smoked off its coal and emptied its fuel tanks. The batteries drained, and the Spacesnake came to its end.

The little snake strung its mechanical shell over three tiny asteroids. It was somewhere deep between two nowheres, but it didn't matter.

The little snake climbed out of the head of the Spacesnake and sat down glumly, feeling very alone.

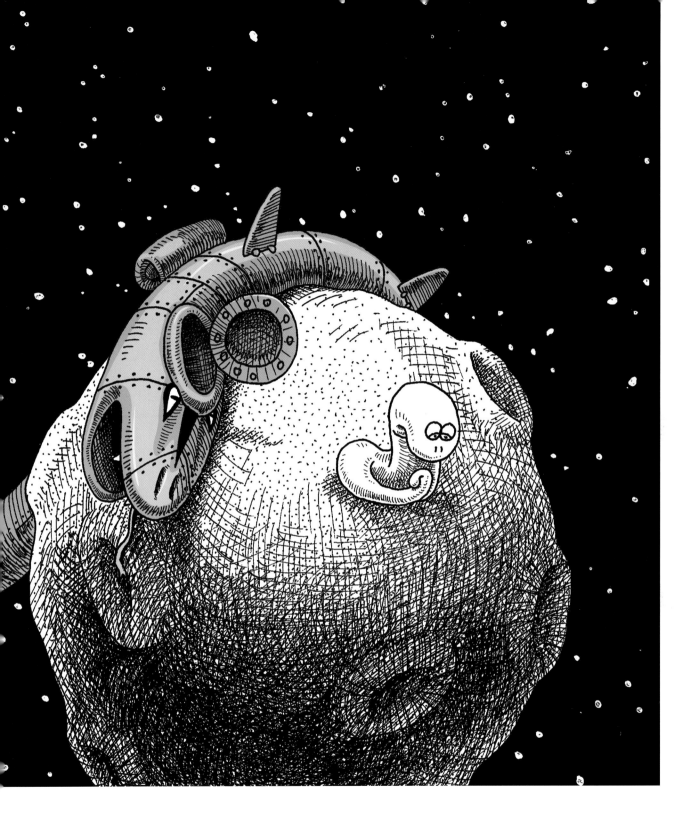

He curled his tiny tail and, with sorrowful thoughts, he hung his head. He felt bad for what he had done.

And that is just the way it *should* be.

The End.

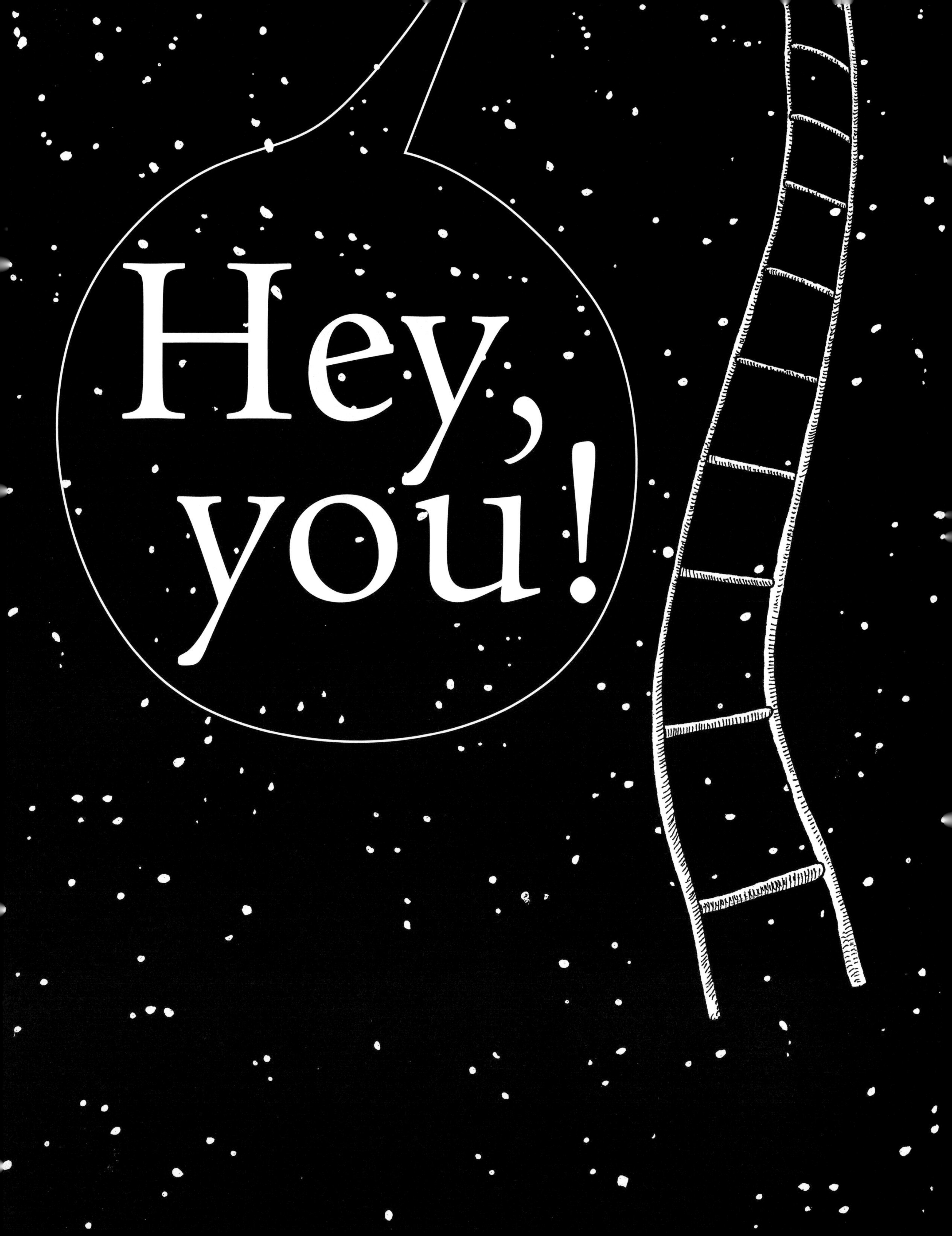
Hey, you!